The Legend of the
Lost Dutchman's Gold Mine

By

Charles H. Huckabay

This book is a work of non-fiction. Names and places have been changed to protect the privacy of all individuals. The events and situations are true.

ISBN: 1-4107-7592-5 (e-book)
ISBN: 1-4107-7591-7 (Paperback)

This book is printed on acid free paper.

1stBooks – rev. 09/02/03

TABLE OF CONTENTS

FOREWARD

In the vast Sonoran wasteland, about twenty miles east of Phoenix, mighty granite mountains rise some four thousand feet above the desert floor. The Superstitions are the center of mystery and legend, tales that date from the Conquestidor to the lone miner and his burro. Today, it is said that these legends, old maps, and stone tablets hold the keys to hidden treasures.

Many have tried, and more than a few have lost their lives, in their search for the secrets of these forboding mountains. Still others have adapted and distorted history in their attempts to tell the stories of the Spanish mines and the Dutchman's lost gold.

Here, in these pages, I will guide you through the path of history and present to you, now, the lost mines of the past.......uncovered!

CHAPTER I

SPANISH CONQUEST

A quiet fascination has troubled me for the past thirty-five years. As a boy, I lived in Chandler, Arizona. In the early 50's all the mountains in Arizona seemed remarkably close, as there was no air pollution. I was always able to look at the Superstition Mountains and make mental notes of obvious landmarks.

By 1955, my father bought a new home in Apache Junction. It was at this time I met Barney Bernard, the author of a book about the Superstition Mountains and the Lost Dutchman Mine. My father was doing some construction work on Barney's home and I was helping him. This gave me the opportunity to enjoy several long talks with Barney. He first introduced me to the legend of the Lost Dutchman Mines.

By 1957, I was making many trips into the Superstitions which lasted several days. I learned the different canyons and their names: First Water, Wiskey Springs, etc. I also learned the many trails with their Spanish names. I have spent many years learning about and finding different places in the Superstitions and have developed a great love for the mountains that has lasted until this day.

In this book I will share with you many of the mysteries which I have uncovered, from the early Spanish conquest to the Dutchman and beyond. Because Barney Bernard shared his secrets with me, I also will share mine with you in hopes you may come to appreciate the rich history and beauty of the Superstition Mountains.

From between the twin peaks of Popocateptl and Ixtaclhuatl, the Spaniard gazed down upon the valley below. The year was 1519 and the moment marked the first time Spanish eyes had ever beheld the city of Tenochtitan, the site of the mighty Aztec nation.

Within the massive stone walls, the ancient Indian civilization flourished. In the fields below, corn, beans, tomatoes, and squash grew abundantly. Tanned leather and beautiful cotton textiles were being traded in the marketplace. The buildings exhibited a mastery of the arts of carpentry and masonry. But, amidst all the majestic splendor, the vision that embedded itself into the mind of Hernando Cortez was that of the exquisitly crafted models of birds and fish...for they were solid gold! Riches, all to be claimed for his motherland.

The fact that the Aztecs, under the rule of Montezuma II, forced tribute, as well as occasional human sacrifices, from the neighboring tribes was, undoubtably, reason enough for Cortez to find them easy allies. In 1521, Cortez led his Spanish troops, aided by these vengeful, rival tribes, to topple the Aztec empire. Montezuma II was killed, the great city destroyed, and the survivors made subject to Spanish rule.

By 1522, a new city stood upon the once sacred ground of Tenochtitan. Under the guidance of Cortez, now governor, it would grow into what is now known as Mexico City. In 1535, Spain declared Mexico a viceroyalty, and to encourage settlement and Christianization, began the practice of bestowing land grants. Noblemen, military men, and the church landowners were entrusted with these responsibilities. At the same time and with great zeal, they began to ravage the land of its mineral wealth, sending the spoils back to Spain.

In 1536, another explorer, Cabeza de Vaca, was sailing home after traveling with Panfilo de Narvaez to Florida. Tragedy struck and Vaca found himself, along with three other shipmates, the only surviviors as their vessel wrecked onto the coast of present day Texas.

The small band trekked through what is now New Mexico to finally reach the Spanish frontier of Mexico. With them they brought stories of great cities of gold lying in the land to the north. The people began to wonder if the old Spanish legend of the seven cities of gold, in the lost region of Cibola, were really true.

Evidently, Spain thought so, for in 1539, Fray Marcos de Ninza was sent to claim the prize. Within the year he returned, reporting findings of only villages made of mud. But Spain would not be denied. It still felt the seven cities were there, somewhere, just waiting to be taken.

Next, Francisco Vasquez Coronado would venture out and for two years, 1540-1542, trod the lands of New Mexico and Arizona; only to reluctantly return, discouraged and empty handed.

In the 1590's, Spain did finally accomplish several things in the person of Juan de Oñate. Early in the decade, Oñate claimed the lands of Arizona for Spain and later let settlers into New Mexico. History tells us this was all done in the name of the Roman Catholic Church. But, to say that conversion of the natives was their only priority does not explain the fact that Oñate had ordered that heavy

4

mining tools, forges, bellows and crucibles for smelting also be taken along. Also interesting is the fact that Oñate, not Spain, carried the financial responsibility of the expedition. It is the inevitable conslusion that, at least to Oñate, this was not simply a holy mission.

In 1598, Oñate, two hundred soldiers, missionaries, and their families settled into northern New Mexico and founded the village of San Juan de los Caballeros, present day San Juan. On their push through the land, Onate's soldiers conquered several tribes of Plains and Navaho Indians, but the diverse bands of Apaches were resisting with a fervor. These battles continued for several years and began to take a toll on the new pilgrims.

Finally, in 1609, Pedro de Peralta was named governor of New Mexico by Spain and sent to relocate the settlers to a more secure area. By 1610, he had succeeded in moving them south of San Juan, founding the new village of Santa Fe.

As the office of governor was more than merely a title of respect, it now fell upon Peralta to divide the land among the people and enforce Spanish rule. Also upon Peralta carried the sole control of trade and commerce. In the years to follow, the Peralta family would, literally, write their names into the legends of the Superstition Mountains of Arizona.

As the Spaniards and Indians fought for possession of New Mexico, the legends of the Superstitions were in genesis. By 1692, the name of Father Kino, a Jesuit priest, was known throughout most of the Indian villages of southernmost Arizona, for he had been traveling the land, converting the red heathen with a passion.

Just south of what is now Tucson, he ventured into a peaceful Papago village, which the natives called Bac. Early on in Father Kino's life, he had dedicated himself to the Church and the memory of Father Xavier, a missionary to the Indian. He christened the village San Xavier del Bac. Kino began bringing the natives into the fold and, by 1697, the village had gained a population of eight-hundred thirty Indians, all living in one-hundred, seventy-six houses. At this time, Father Kino began to introduce cattle into the area and founded a modest ranch. On April 28, 1700, the construction of a church began.

It should be noted that the Roman Catholic Church, at this time, held powerful influence with the Spanish government. Along with their Christian aspects, they had become a mighty militant group. The drive for new souls was equalled only by the lust for gold, silver, and other precious metals of the earth. The riches would all be sent to the mother church in Spain in order to attain the wealth needed to maintain its power.

In the years to follow, other priests would join Father Kino and later take up where he would leave off. The enslaving of the Indian converts to work the land and mine new found ore became common practice among the priests. Soon they would sift their way northward toward the Gila River and the Superstition Mountains.

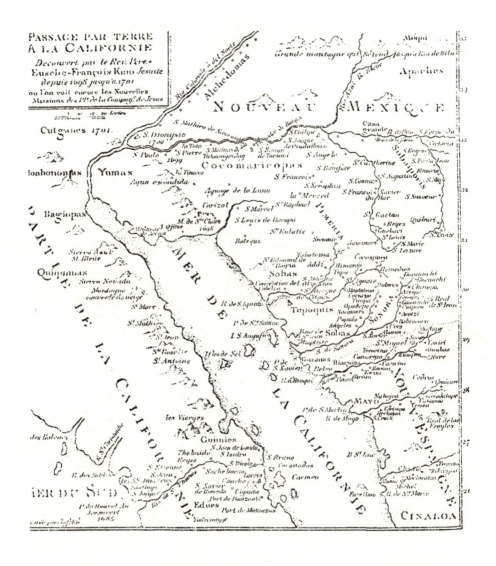

PASSAGE PAR TERRE
À LA CALIFORNIE
Decouvert par le Rev. Pere.
Eusebe-François Kino Jesuite
depuis 1698 jusqu'à 1701
ou l'on voit encore les Nouvelles
Missions de la Pd. de la Compag.ᵉ de Jesus

Though many "historical experts" claim the Jesuit invasion did not reach into the Superstition Mountains and the surrounding area until the early 1800's, one can plainly see by the dates on Father Kino's map that mission activity and exploration had been established by 1701.

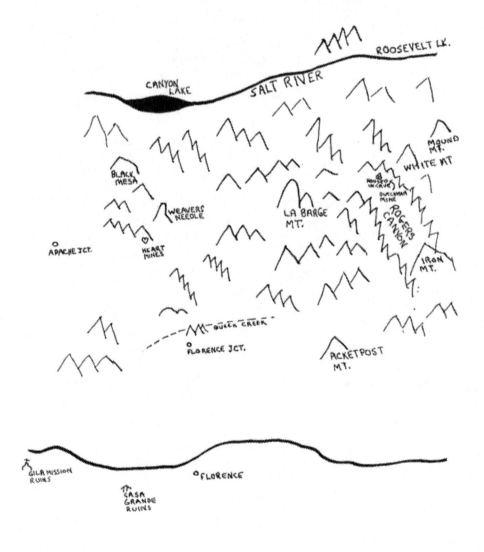

The amazing story that follows is one that has never before been told. It contains the seed of the Peralta Heart Mine legend. The exact dates cannot be confirmed and the names have long since been forgotten. We shall let the facts, which we have uncovered, stand as evidence to the authenticity of the story.

Sometime in the early 17th century, the Jesuit missionaries did reach the Gila River. In the days when its waters flowed unrestricted, they found, in the area now known as Blackwater, a small tribe of Pima farmers. There, on the southern side of the river, about fifteen miles west of what is now Florence, they erected their mission.

Life would have remained simple for the contented villagers had it not been for the trained eyes of the priest. Surely, the hand crafted Indian art caught his eye. To the natives, jewelry and talismans; but, the silver trinkets promised wealth for the church.

Questioned as to the source of this material, the naive people pointed to the northeast, into the Superstition Mountains. Soon the Jesuit Father had learned the exact location and the news sent back to Spain along the network of missions. Shortly thereafter, other priests arrived and the Pimas, too, found themselves on a holy mission, bound in slavery to work the mines in the name of religion.

Fifteen miles northeast of the village, in a canyon running east and west, they began to pick their way into what is now called Dacite Cliffs. On a ledge high above the workings, a huge, heart shaped rock sat, overlooking the industrious group below. In latter years, this rock would become one of the most sought after landmarks of the Superstition legends.

Below, water oozed its way from the bottom of the cliff to form a freshwater spring, traces of which are still quite evident today. It was here the priests made camp, erecting arrastres and smelters. As the days passed by, other veins were discovered and were beginning to be worked; but, something unseen was about to occur, something so horrible it was never spoken of afterwards.

The fate of the mining camp, its priests, and the little Gila mission may never be exactly known. Today, the mission lies in ruin, only the front wall with its belltower remain. It appears out of place as its Spanish architecture towers above the Indian community which surrounds it. The federal land, its inhabitants, and its no trespassing signs keep the curious away. The natives refuse to comment on whatever stories may have been handed down.

Despite the silence and secrets, other historic events of the period may hold the clues to his mystery; for from them, two possible conclusions may be drawn.

In the year 1751, the enslaved Papagos of San Xavier del Bac revolted, the priests were murdered, and the mission destroyed. The Pimas of the Gila mission and mining camp also may have rebelled against the iron fist of their Jesuit masters. The other possible conclusion may have also been caused by the San Xavier rebellion. The word of the massacre and reports of Jesuit missionaries enslaving the Indians to engage in a mining frenzy h ad finally brought action from the Spanish government. In 1767, Carlos III ordered the Jesuits to cease and desist, then expelled them from the new frontier. Upon this decree, the mission could have been abandoned and left to ruin. But this seems highly unlikely as it is not human nature of Spanish policy of the times to leave any source of wealth to remain dormant.

Of the two possibilities we lean to the more tragic and violent because of the dark shroud of mystery and intrigue covering the mission today. In either event, the mine soon fell into obscurity, still laced with its precious metals.

About twenty miles west of Florence, Arizona, on the south side of the Gila River, the remains of this old mission still stand. Another silent testimony to the Jesuit activity of the 1700's which has long been either forgotten or denied.

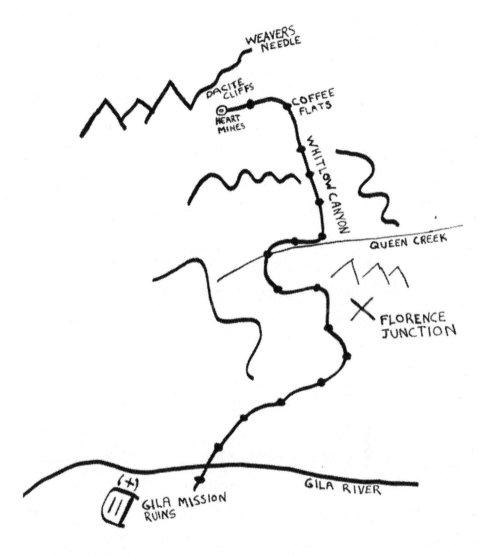

Following the Indian revolts of 1751, the Superstion Mountains returned to the wilderness as in ages past. It's rugged terrain now scarred by the Spanish digging, which now lay dormant. In the desert below, amidst rubble and ruin, the front wall of the Gila mission stood, ominously for all to see.

Charles H. Huckabay

While the northern boundaries of the Sonoran Desert lay unchallanged, Spanish rule began pushing it's way into new territories in the east. 1763 marked the end of the French and Indian War, in which Spain had gained all lands west of the Mississippi River. Thinking that the eastern conflicts had now been settled, Spain could once again turn it's attention back to the mineral wealth of the Gila River region. But, before any treasure dared to be claimed, the task of dealing with the inhabitants had to be dealt with. This chore fell upon the Franciscan missionaries.

The Franciscans were by no means new to the missionary fields of the northern territories. From the days of Oñate, they had been converting the tribes of southern New Mexico with much success. So, with a proven plan of action, they stepped into the paths of their Jesuit predecessors. With kindness and devotion, they won the respect of the Papago Indians and by 1763, re-established the village of San Xavier del Bac

But still, peace was not to be had. From the north, groups of marading Gila Apaches began to make lightning raids, stealing cattle, crops, women and children. Behind, they left only death and suffering.

Another obstacle had been placed between Spain and the fortune beyond the Gila. In 1768, Spanish runners, traveling by foot, arrived at the mission of Arizpe, the capital of Sonora. With them, they brought news from Chihuahua; Father Francisco Garces was to arrive shortly. He was requesting a meeting with the runners from the outlying missions and a council with his fellow priests.

Spain and the Roman Catholic Church had commisioned the father to assess and evaluate the situation; then, to take the necessary steps to bring it under control.

When Father Garces finally arrived, the news he received was much worse than he had anticipated. The villages were under constant threat of Apache raids and the priests dared not venture on past San Xavier. Drastic measures had to be taken soon or more lives would be lost and the northern crusade would be in vain.

CHAPTER II

THE PERALTAS

By the mid 1700's, the descendants of Governor Pedro Peralta had grown to great social and economic stature. They had inherited the choice pasturelands near Santa Fe, which he had laid claim to while still governor of the new province. Clansmen is Sonora, also, had built an empire of cattle ranches.

To maintain just one cow and calf on the sparse desert land, it necessitated one square mile of pasture per year to feed them. By todays standards, these ranches would be considered huge, for huge they would have to be to maintain a large family and turn a profit. To these large rancheros, the Church made their proposal.

As payment, to recruit the crucial aid needed to overcome it's deadly obstacles, the Church offered the locations to their abandoned mines. The Peraltas were to furnish armed support to the missions and laborers for the mines. In turn, the Church would settle for the tithes paid upon the gains. And Spain, as usual, would collect it's mandatory two-thirds. Without hesitation the Paraltas grasped the opportunity, and leaving behind only those necessary to the ranches upkeep, headed north to San Xavier, loaded with arms supplies, and mining equipment.

Once reaching San Xavier, members of the band were assigned for mission support and the dons then received the instructions that were to lead them to the mines in the land beyond.

Following the directions from the priests, the Peraltas mining expedition struck out. Runners were sent ahead scouting for the landmarks and signs that were to lead them on to their final destination. Within the week, they had reached the Gila mission ruins and faced their first real threat, the Pima Indians.

Though reasonably weary of these new invaders, the Indians knew they would be no match for the superior weapons of the tresspassers. They, too, had suffered at the hands of the Apache bands and the last thing they now needed was another enemy to battle. The Peraltas, also, had no reason to fight if the natives would let them pass in peace. So, parley was held and a truce was found to be advantagous. The Peraltas gained rite of passage and the Pimas, a new ally against the Apache.

Free again to move on, the band crossed the Gila River a few miles east of the old mission ruins. Heading northeast, they reached the Superstition foothills and once there, made camp for the night.

The next day, they awoke for what would be the last and final leg of their journey. They began by winding their way around the mountains near present-day Florence Junction. Northward, ever working northward, they traveled through the rugged, treacherous canyons. Runners were again sent forth. The hot, dry air hung in the canyons and the terrain seemed barren of shade. At this point many must have thought of turning back for the safety and tranquility of their Sonoran homelands. But after a time, the runners returned. Eagerly, they gave their report; the priests had not lied, for they had seen the mines which lay only a short distance away.

The runners lead the group ahead, up the canyon to where it junctioned with another, larger canyon running east and west. Here, they turned west, hugging the southern walls of a huge mountain. It's sheer cliffs reached up, over two-thousand feet to meet the blue, cloudless sky. They followed the mountain about three miles, until the cliffs made a sharp, northerly turn.

As the Don's and their men followed the runners and rounded the bend, they stopped, gazing in awe into the cliffs beyond. About one-hundred yards beyond, on a ledge about two-hundred feet above them, the huge, heart-shaped rock sat, just as the priests had described it. Below this stone, where the mountain met the canyon floor, one mine entrance was already visible.

At the base of the cliff, to the left of the mine, water oozed from the cliff to form a pool of fresh, spring water. Here, the Peraltas set up base camp and the next few days were spent locating other openings and preparing for the work ahead. The year was 1768.

In the years 1768 through the early 1800's, wordly events proved well for Spain and the Peraltas. In 1779, Spain helped the United States break it's ties with Great Britain; Santa Fe became a great trade center, and by 1797, the Church had rebuilt a magnificent mission at San Xavier del Bac. Through all of this, the Peraltas were gaining wealth by picking their way through the Superstition cliffs.

In 1810, things took a turn for the worse. The peasants in Mexico were revolting, making trade with Spain difficult. The only other outlet for commerce lay miles to the northeast, in the town of Santa Fe. The sole route available to the Sonoran ranches ran east to Chihuahua, then due north through El Paso. Unfortunately for the

Sonorans, the Chihuahuan merchants and ranches held a monopoly over the commerce along this trail with which the southwestern ranches could not compete. A definate delima: the revolution had cost them nearby markets and the Santa Fe option was too costly.

In 1780, the New Mexican governor, Juan Bastista de Anza, had tried to find a more direct route between Santa Fe and Arizpe: but the waterless New Mexican desert, through which he passed, proved too long and difficult.

The Peraltas, now fairly familiar with the Superstition regions, opened to themselves another option. They had kinsmen near Santa Fe who possessed vast acres of pastureland. Beyond the mining camps, to the north, the Rio Salado River flowed through the rugged terrain from New Mexico. It would be very profitable if a route could be found through the Superstitions, between the Gila and Rio Salado Rivers.

Out of this necessity, a trail was glazed; from Sonora, north to the Gila, then around the western end of the mountains. On this route they could reach the Rio Salado, which they would then follow east into New Mexico. The trail was long and dangerous, but the Peralta vaccaros soon proved it not impossible.

During the next ten years, heards of horses were brought up from the Sonoran ranches and pastured on the Peralta ranges of New Mexico. Though trade with the new American settlers in Missouri was outlawed by Spain, the black market had become a booming success. The Peralta family began to gain more wealth from their horse trading than from working the earth, for Spain and the Church got no percentage from the black market.

In 1821, two events occured that would push the horse market into a frenzy. Mexico declared its independence from Spain and trade with any and all foreigners was legalized by the newly formed government.

The Peraltas now desired a faster, more direct route to Santa Fe. Once more, runners were sent out from the mining camps, this time to explore deep into the heart of the Superstition range. Within the year, a new path was discovered.

The new horse trail ran from Sonora to the Gila, as before, but once at the river it picked up the old mining trail northeast to Queen Creek. Still following the old trail along the creek, they would travel a short distance to what would now be the trails junction. At this point, the mining trail spun due north, up a canyon, to the mines. The horse trail continued on, following Queen Creek northeast, zig-zagging through the mountains for about four miles. In what is now known as Hewitt Canyon, they went north another few miles, then climbed a mountain range and proceeded down into a long canyon running north. Keeping to this canyon for about seven miles, they would eventually emerge on the southern bank of the Rio Salado. Upon reaching the river, it would be an easy task driving the herds east to New Mexico, and once there, leading them across the river to graze in the pastures on the northern side.

Water seemed to be the largest concern, but this was easily overcome by the ingenious Mexicans. At crucial points, catch basins were fashioned from crude cement made from earth and stones. The walls were built on the mountains' sides to catch and hold the rainfall as it traveled down the slopes and through the rocks.

The revolutions in Mexico continued, but business in Santa Fe seemed as though it would never peak. As it continously rose, the Peraltas made plans to move all their holdings to New Mexico, not a small task for the mighty dons. While Chihuahua still held tight reign over trade on the trail from northeastern Mexico, the Peraltas now had a quick route of their own. Herds of up to fifty horses were to be pushed along the rocky trail through the mountains.

In time, the horse and mining trails were worn deep into the land. Trail markers were cut into cactus and stones were carved into rock maps. At the trails junction, near Florence Junction, stone markers were carved and erected. Their two faces commemorated the two seperate events: the re-opening of the mines by the dons and the horse trail through the mountains.

In 1828, while driving one of the herds through the long northerly canyon, gold was discovered in a stream that flowed from one of the subtary canyons on the eastern side. Exploration soon followed and it was discovered that one of the canyons cliffs contained a very large vein of gold.

Quickly, the dons secretly dispatched a small mining expedition to the area. Soon, they had reached the canyon, confirmed the find, and begun to dig.

Because of the threat of the nearby Apache bands, the mining groups were small and worked quietly. To their favor, the narrow canyon was a fortress in itself. When scouting for the gold's source, the Mexicans had found, on the opposite side of the canyon, the perfect location to build their shelter. A long, natural opening had been found, directly under an overhanging rock. It was about thirty feet long, six feet high, and ten feet deep. At the back of this cave, to one side, fresh spring water trickled from the rock. From the cave, one could see into the mouth of their mine.

The men went to work building walls for what would soon be their home and fort. Utilizing tree limbs, stones, and mud, the walls were soon finished. The entrance was located near the center with gun ports bordering each side. The whole shelter seemed inpenitrable. With this completed, they returned to the chore of mining the ore with a sense of security.

Following the gold-laden rose quartz, they dug their way into the mountain. After digging several feet into the cliff, the vein widened into a leadge of gold and quartz about eighteen inches wide. Fearing that the shaft might collapse if they were to enlarge it, they decided to begin a new shaft in the slope above and tunnel down into the vein. Thus, they began the slow and tedious work of digging a new shaft.

As the gold began to be extracted in volume, another fear had to be dealt with. As supplies arrived, so did the rumors that American trappers and other treasure seekers were in the area. Also, Apache sightings were becoming more frequent. Measures needed to be taken to protect the told until it could be safely moved to Santa Fe.

Along the rocky canyon floor, the winter rains had cut a deep and rugged path into the earth. Along it's course, even deeper pits had been formed, so deep in fact, that they were still pooled with water in midsummer. These pools became the deposit pits for the Peralta gold as the ore was let to sink to their bottoms. Small lightning raids or theives in the night were no longer a threat. If anyone now sought to take their treasure from them, the raiders would have to stand and fight.

While the years passed, the Peralta family was amassing a fortune, unaware of the horror that lay just ahead.

In 1836, the Texas settlers revolted and won their independence from Mexico. 1841 marked the year the Americans first attempted to take Santa Fe and gain control of the trade center. By 1846, the New Mexican armies were dwindling because of a great apathy covering the people. The Mexican government learned that the Americans were again marching toward Santa Fe. To fire up the New Mexican people and manipulate them to battle, the Mexican government began to spread rumors of the ruthless Americans. Butchers, they were called, who would torture the men, rape their women, and defile their churches. Though intended to stir the people to war, instead, the rumors frightened them into hiding.

The farmers poured into the cities for protection. The rich boarded up their houses and fled into the mountains with all they could carry. The priests had even started to dismantle their churches to prevent their desacration.

The Peraltas, also caught up in the panic, abandoned their ranch and took to the mountains. But they, unlike the others, had already chosen their sanctuary: the site of the gold mines, now known as Las Minas Sombrero.

In 1846, General Kearny, leading an American force, entered Santa Fe. No shots were fired and no one resisted. The small Mexican army that had been stationed nearby had been ordered to give no resistance. Tidy sums, paid to high-ranking government officials, were rumored the cause.

When the news that Santa Fe had been taken reached the Peraltas, they sensed all was lost; their huge empire gone. Already, American eyes were on the silver mines to the west. Shortly, they too would have to be deserted.

The push was on. The Peraltas would mine as much of the precious metals that they could in the next few months, load their treasure, and escape back to Sonora, then perhaps on to Spain.

Throughout the Superstition range, many new mines were opened and worked out. Camps were built, other cave fortresses established, and crops were planted. Though Apache bands were seen frequently, their small numbers appeared as no threat to the Mexicans. As they worked and lived in this cruel, savage land the months became years.

In 1848, more disappointment befell the little mountain communities. The Treaty of Guadalupe had been signed. In it, Spain had ceeded all lands north of the Gila River to the United States. With the Americans already prospecting the western boundaries of the Superstitions, the Peraltas reluctantly made the decision to close out the mines in that area. They hurriedly packed their animals and headed east, along the old horse trail, toward the safety of Las Minas Sombrero. Behind, the old stone maps and trail markers received their final etchings and because they were too heavy to be taken along, were hidden close to where the trail markers had stood.

Meanwhile, the Apaches had been forced deeper into the mountains by the white man. Their raids became less frequent on the desert villages and their only hope for survival lay in keeping the inner mountains free of invaders. They began to mass in number as the result of being pushed into a smaller area. Threatened now by the Peralta invasion, the Apaches made one quick sweep and cleaned their homeland.

As the sun set that evening, the Peralta treasure returned to the mountains. Many tried to flee the savage onslaught the barrage of arrows and black-market bullets, only to find themselves lost in the unknown regions of the vast wilderness. The Indians, thinking they had done an efficient job, then went about the task of covering the mines. Los Minas Sombrero was to be forgotten forever. But, unknown to the Apache, a small handful of Mexicans had escaped the massacre, at least two of which would someday return.

The Peralta Stone Maps and their trail of "eighteen places".

left to right: Hoyt Huckabay author, view looking back towards trail head, burro pen, rock house

left to right: rock house (2 left pictures), view from hole in rock house

left to right: view from hole in rock house, view from hole in rock house looking towards where cave was located, entrance to a cave

left to right: Dennis standing in cave, Dennis exploring cave, view from cave looking towards rock house, notice overhang (2 right pictures)

CHAPTER III

THE DUTCHMAN

In the early 1800's, Obershwandorf was one of a few villages that composed the Slabian state of Wurttenburg. Now part of present-day Germany, its tiny parish houses the records of it's past populace. Here, within the musty storeroom, the following can be confirmed: on August 3, 1808, born to Johann and Anna Walz, a son, his given name….Jakob Walz.

Amidst the dense mountain landscapes of the Black Forest, the child grew to maturity. The family business being that of clothmaking, he learned the trade; unaware that the roots of a legend were about to take hold.

In 1835, the Duke of Wurttenburg mystified and enthused his countrymen with his exploits in a far off land. His book aroused many to seek their futures in the exotic lands of the North Americas. Perhaps it was this stirred curiousity that led Jakob Walz to leave his native land…perhaps not. In 1839, at the age of thirty-one, Walz set foot on American soil. However, behind in Germany, he had not sought the mandatory permission from the German Magistrait to migrate. Precise records, listing all those receiving this permission, were kept. The name of Jakob Walz appears in none of these, nor is there any other document, including marriage or death, to attest of any further life in Germany after his birth.

In America, the German, "Jakob Walz" became Jacob Waltz. to accomidate English pronunciation. With this done, he resided in Baltimore, Maryland for two years. Then in 1841, he moved to New Jersey to work for a cousin who operated a tannery. There, the news of gold strikes in North Carolina began to reach his ears. Contemplating a quick fortune, he arrived in the gold fields of Meadow Creek, but to his frustration, he was too late, so, he moved onward to Georgia.

On November 12, 1848, the same year as the Peralta massacre, Waltz was formaly declaring his desire to become a U.S. citizen. This, he announced by letter to the Adams County Courthousein Natchez, Mississippi. However, a delay of his naturalization was forced when news of new gold strikes in California reached Mississippi, for he joined a wagon train and moved west.

Weeks later, upon reaching California, he found the new frontier already overrun with prospectors and adventure seekers. It seemed impossible for the late arrivals to find anything more than work on the already established claims. Reluctantly, Waltz took a job working for Rubin Blackey, who had begun pulling gold ore from the San Grabriel Canyon.

The territorial census of 1860 recorded Waltz as a day laborer on July 24 at the Azusa Township, County of Los Angles. One year later, July 19, 1861, while still in Los Angles County, he received official notification that he had gained the U.S. citizenship which he had sought in 1848.

The year of 1862 brought about two major events that were to play heavily upon the future of Jacob Waltz. News of other gold strikes was first. It was now being discovered along the Gila River in the New Mexican Territory of Arizona. But if these new finds were not enough to tempt Waltz eastward, the second event surely sealed his fate.

The California rains of 1862 caused flooding so great, nearly every mining camp in San Gabriel County was destroyed. The devastation was so overwhelming, they would never be rebuilt.

Waltz, now jobless and with no promise of a future in California, joined with a small band of men and headed for Arizona. Panning and picking their way along, he and four other prospectors finally staked their first claims. On September 21, 1863, in Yavapai County, just south of Prescott, they filed on the Gross Lode.

The lack of quartz mills in the area left the men holding titles to unworkable claims and the still very active Apache made it difficult even for placer workers. In fact, the Indian raids became so frequent that in 1864, Waltz and several others sent a petition to Governor John N. Goodman, asking for military protection.

While the Territorial Census of May, 1864 found Waltz still in the area, others were either selling out or simply abandoning their claims. Many had not the heart to stand against the Apache or the patience to await the construction of the quartz mills. Soon, Waltz too abandoned his claim and moved on, southwest, with two others, Joseph Smith and Peter Backens.

The three treasure seekers next settled on the Big Rebel Lode in the Walnut Grove Mining District and on September 14, 1864, they filed their claims. On December 27, 1865, Waltz and Backens filed again, this time on the General Grant Lode, about twenty-five miles southwest of Prescott. These claims were lost because the men did not comply with the mandatory annual assessment. For whatever reason the two might have had for letting their claims elapse, the future would prove the General Grant Lode very fertile. It later became the site of the famous Black Queen Mine, producing thousands of dollars in gold ore.

But Waltz had moved on, for in 1868, now sixty years of age, he arrived in the Salt River Valley and set about homesteading one-hundred sixty acres north of the Salt River. The land, which is now covered by the Phoenix Airport, was assessed for four-hundred dollars in improvements the first year Waltz settled in; no small amount for the time.

At the same time, vast irrigation systems were beginning to be developed, with the result of vast numbers of Mexicans migrating into the area from Sonora. They had come seeking work as farm laborers. Nine such laborers dwelled within the boundaries of Waltz's homestead.

The interesting fact to be noted here is that the Territorial Census has recorded the name of one of the laborers as Peralta. It is possible Waltz learned the story of the old Spanish mines from a descendant of the original discoverers. In any case, something drew Waltz, at age sixty-one, into the Superstition Mountains.

The late fall of 1870 found Waltz leaving his homestead in the care of his Mexican tennants and, once again, on the move. On this venture, he paired with another German immigrant by the name of

Jacob Weiser. New to the territory, Weiser had been a carpenter by trade until his unscrupulous dealings with the public forced him into moving on in search of other means of income. He had come to Arizona to seek its mineral wealth, and soon, the two men had entered into a prospecting pact. Their common fear of the Apache was the force that bound them together.

Outfitted only with two pack mules, they entered the Superstition Mountains from the southwestern end of the range, picked up the Queen Creek, and worked their way east. Utilizingthe creek as their guide, they plunged deeper and deeper into the rugged mountains. They stopped occassionally to pan for traces of precious minerals. Then they would move on again, unaware they were trodding the trail blazed by the Peralta family many years before.

Soon, they made their way over a long range of mountains, then down into a long canyon below. Once in the canyon, they began to work north, panning its narrow stream. About five miles along, they found a subtary canyon sweeping in from the east. Choosing to explore its possibilities before heading on north, they led their burros along its rocky and densely wooded floor. At once they were bordered by sheer cliffs and sharp slopes that reached up, ever so high, to form towering peaks and jagged outlines against the evening sky. The setting sun cast it's light across the canyon, tossing shades and color upon the twisted, ancient landscape. The two men took it all in, breathlessly, unaware that here, in this place, formed millions of years before by volcanicupheavals, all their hopes, all their dreams....and all their fears would be realized. Worn and weary, Waltz and Weisner camped for the night. Their dread of being in Apache territory forced from them the temptation of lighting a campfire to comfort them from the cool night air. They burrowed deep into their sleeping bags and waited for sleep to overcome the chill.

The next morning, they awoke and, seeking water, approached the creek. The savage rains had cut deep into the canyon's floor. Huge boulders and deep pits lay in the course of the now gentle stream. If they were to make plans to stay in this area any length of time, they knew they would have to pitch camp on higher ground to protect themselves from the flash floods of which the signs were to emminant. Waltz, being a veteran prospector, also realized that these pits were perfect catch basins. Gold and silver which might have eroded from the mountains and washed downstream would, eventually, find their way to settle into the basins.

Shortly, they had lowered a bucket on a rope to the bottom of one of the pits. At a depth of about ten feet, they scooped sand and sediment from it's floor. Partially full, the pail raced to break the water's surface. Above, it's contents were poured out to form a glistening little pile. Content after several pails had been hauled up, they began sifting through the sand and rock, planning to pan it out in the little stream. But today, their pans would never touch water.

As they began fingering through the piles, small golden flakes in the sand began to flicker in the sun's rays. Small, B-B size stones were discovered to be pure gold. The two men stood, and while clutching their treasure in their hands, gazed down into the pit below. At the pit's bottom, beneath the top layer of dirt and sand, they knew a fortune waited.

They began to make preparations for an extended stay. Because of the Apaches and the fear of flash-flooding, a permanant campsite had to be found in the higher elevations of the canyon. They began to search the landscape for this safe, secure location. It was then they discovered the walls of the old cave dwelling. High up in the face of the northern cliffs, the old Spanish fort, still very much intact.

Cautiously, they climbed to the opening of the dwelling, weapons in hand. The open doorway was situated directly center of two walls, extending twenty feet in opposite directions. Near the top of both walls, midway down, windows approximately eighteen inches square overlooked the only two paths leading up to the fort.

Waltz lunged through the doorway, weilding his weapon left to right, ready to fire upon anything that moved. The cave was empty, without sign of any current habitation. After Weiser received the all-clear, both began assessing the cave's potential. A partition of stones divided the cave's interior into two rooms of equal size. The rooms were about five feet high and their ceilings slanted to the back about eight feet to a height of two feet. In the room on the left, water trickled from the back wall to form a small pool of fresh water within the room. Looking out the two windows, they found they could see a great distance down both ends of the canyons. Perfect. The cave would become their base camp, providing both protection from the weather and a fort in the event they were attacked by the maurading Apaches.

Below the dwelling, at the base of the canyon, they found a large boulder with an overhang on one side. Here, under the stone roof, they formed a burro pen by stacking up stones to form a wall. A large tree limb was utilized for a gate. This would serve two purposes, one, it would shelter the animals. Two, if anyone or anything came too near, the burros would surely cry out and alert them to the impending danger.

Next, all supplies were carried up to the house in the cave and stored. The burros were fed and watered and placed in the newly erected pen. With this done, and the night quickly approaching, the two settled into the safety of their mountain fortress and rested the night.

The next day, more plans were made. Rather than finger and pan through the bucket loads of sand, which first must be hauled from the bottom of the pits, Waltz and Weiser decided to take the gold from the preceeding days venture and journey to Florence for supplies and better equipment for extracting the gold.

As no other prospectors had as yet ventured as deep into the Superstitions, and because filing a claim would surely cause a rush once the assay was recorded, Waltz and Weiser agreed to keep their discovery a secret. Believing all would be safe until their return, they packed their burros and headed for town.

After two days of slow and cautious traveling, they reached the small settlement of Florence. There, they contacted a carpenter, now known only as "Frank", and contracted for two dry-washers to be built. When "Frank" completed his task, he was paid for his services with a gold nugget. The storekeeper, from whom Waltz and Weiser purchased their supplies, was also paid with a similar stone. With business now complete, the two disappeared back into the mountains.

Upon their return to camp, they now felt a new problem had to be dealt with. Surely, people in Florence must have marveled at their high grade ore…would they attempt to follow? Along with the constant fear of the Apache, they now had to worry about white thieves and cut-throats. Dangers, all too real, began to play on their minds.

In the days that followed, Waltz and Weiser continued, anxiously about their work. The dry washers were utilized in the daytime, then at evening, they were hidden among the bushes. All seemed to be going unexpectedly well. Each night, just before retiring, Waltz stood at the entrance of the cave. He gazed down through the trees and bushes at the stream below and watched as the setting sun glistened off the golden flakes that still lay unclaimed on the bottom of the now disturbed pool. Then, as the sun disappeared behind the western mountains, he would withdraw to the comfort of his bedroll and prepare for the following day's work.

On a fateful day in 1848, two Mexican laborers had fled in terror when their mining camp was overrun by savage Apache bands.

Miraculously, they had escaped over the southern mountains and continued on to Sonora, vowing never to return. But now, twenty-three years later, the two had somehow mustered the courage to return and claim the forgotten mine. No map was necessary, as they remembered in exact detail, the trail to "Las Minas Sombrero".

They had followed the Queen Creek and the still visable cactus notched trail which led them into the long, northern canyon. Years before, horses had also been pushed along this route on their way to sale in Santa Fe, but is was gold they sought on this trip. From the northern canyon, they made their way into the subtary canyon to the east.

They had traveled for days and now darkness, once again, was upon them. They had come so far and were too close to stop now, so they continued on in the pale glow of the moon above. Soon, they passed the old treasure pits of the canyon's floor. How much, if any, of the stash still remained was of no concern to them now, for they knew where to get more, faster and easier.

They traveled but a short distance farther, dismounted and climbed the southern slope. When they arrived at the site where they were sure the opening would be, they then discovered the entrance covered with rock and dirt. It was not hard for them to realize that the Indians had covered the entrance hoping to conceal it's secrets for eternity. They also knew it would not be long before they would have it re-opened. Down they climbed, unloading their pick and shovel from their pack animal. Up again, they climbed and confidently began to pick away at the mountain in the dead of night.

Waltz and Weiser had been asleep but a few hours when their peace became interrupted by the sound of steel on stone. Slowly, they made their way toward the blanket that covered the entrance of the house in the cave. They eased the blanket ever so slightly to the side, just enough to peer, curiously, across the canyon to the figures eagerly at work on the other side. Who were these people so busy at work in the middle of the night? Why hadn't the burros awakened them? Waltz and Weiser grabbed their weapons and stealthfully slid down the mountain for a closer look.

The two Mexicans continued digging, oblivious to everything but their own lust for the concealed treasure. Suddenly, one of them broke through the earth to a hollow beneath...a triumph that would be short lived.

Waltz and Weiser had taken dead aim on what appeared to them to be two Apaches. They had made the decision to shoot first and ask questions later. For the first time since the creation of Heaven and Earth, the sound of gunshots echoed through the canyon, rebounding in the mountains beyond. The two Mexicans lay dead only a few feet from the re-opened shaft. They had made their long journey only to meet the fate they had escaped so many years before.

Meanwhile, Waltz and Weiser, realizing what they had done, beat a hasty retreat back to the safety of their cave, least their shots beckon more, unfriendlier intruders. There, they kept watch until daybreak, then satisfied all was safe, ventured out to inspect their kill.

What, if any, animals the two unwelcome strangers may have brought were nowhere to be seen. Perhaps the gunshots had frightened them off. The two Germans climbed the steep slope and were at once shocked to find two dead Mexicans lying, where just previously, they had killed two Apaches. What, in God's name, they thought, were two Mexicans doing at their secret location? The answer to their puzzlement was soon found, there in the mountain where the two strangers had been digging, a small opening was visable.

Relieved that the two invaders had not been Apaches, Waltz and Weiser began to remove more dirt, expanding the opening. They removed gravel, rocks and pieces of wood to enlarge the opening enough for a man to enter. They peered into the hole and saw only darkness, one of them rushed back to the cave dwelling to secure a lantern.

Now armed with lantern and rifle, the two crawled through the opening. Inside, they found the shaft of a long abandoned digging. Down they climbed, the passage angling sharply, making it barely accessible without rope or ladder. The light of the opening disappeared behind and above them. With lanterns lit, they moved deeper into the mountain. They moved their lanterns slowly, in a circle, searching the walls for signs of whatever had drawn the two Mexicans to the location. Their anticipation began to grow as they

Charles H. Huckabay

waved the light before them. As if in answer the walls began to cast the light back…gold!

The floor of the shaft seemed to be embedded with pinhead size gold nuggets and the ceiling contained an enormous vein of the metal mingled with pink quartz.

The two men scurried from the hole enthused and amazed, unaware that just three miles to the northeast, the Mexican pack animal had wandered into an Apache camp.

The tribe had heard the gunplay the preceeding night, but because of the thundering echoes, were unable to discern their true direction. Now the animal, emerging from the canyon, gave them a definate location in which to search. Though primarily concerned with the fertile land to the north, the Apache were not about to let the whiteman take root anywhere in their sacred mountains. They would seek out this threat and eliminate it.

Waltz and Weiser dug the shallow graves for the two who had traveled such a great distance to join their ancestors. As they toiled under the Spring sun, they knew that the approaching summer heat would succeed, where man had failed, in driving them from the mountains. With time growing short and supples dwindling, new strategies were planned.

It was decided that Waltz would return to Florence for supplies and Weiser, meanwhile would work the mine. Upon Waltz's return, both would gather as much of the high-grade ore as their burros could carry and return to civilization to live out the rest of their lives in the lap of luxury.

Very early the next morning, Waltz set out for Florence, his burro carrying but a small quantity of the yellow metal. The two men wished each other well and was Waltz set off, Weiser proceeded to the mine to begin work. As Waltz exited the western end of the canyon a small band of Apache warriors were entering from the east.

Once again Waltz paid for his supplies with gold ore, then beat a hasty retreat before the news of the fabulous rock could spread making it impossible for him to leave privately. He had been away for three days when he re-entered the canyon. Arriving to the point directly between the cave dwelling and the mine, he began sensing something was wrong. The burro pen was empty and Weiser was nowhere about.

First he climbed to the cave dwelling, entered and found it empty. The cooking utensils, Weiser's bedroll and the few remaining supplies were gone. Waltz began to tremble, the golden cache was also missing. Thoughts of abandonment began to race through his head. Had Weiser decided to pack up and light out, keeping to himself all they had both worked so hard to gain?

Waltz, now stricken with anxiety, rushed down the mountain, scrambled across the gulley and began to climb the other side, all the while calling Weiser's name. Perhaps Weiser had simply moved camp to the other side, it was possible. He called out again…but still there was no answer.

Furious now, he reached the opening. At once he was reeled back by the stench in the air. Once again fear replaced anger. Waltz froze…the buzzing of a thousand flies pounded in his ears. He began to realize both, sound and smell, were being emitted from the shaft.

His hand trembled as he pulled his old kerchief from his pocket. Covering his mouth and nose with the rag, he ventured forward. Though he carried no lantern, the sun's light encroached far enough into the opening to allow his fears to become reality. The body of Jacob Weiser lay just inside, Apache arrows protruding from every limb of the mutilated body. Terrified, Waltz panicked. He ran from the mine, stumbled down the mountain side, seized his burro and fled from the canyon.

Waltz reached Florence the next day, exhausted and overcome with grief. Initially he had planned to report the death of his partner, but perhaps, he thought, that would not be so smart. Questions would be asked and he would surely have to divuldge the secret location so Weiser's body might be claimed. Before he said anything, he needed time to re-coop, time to think things out more clearly.

Unfortunately, he had not entered Florence un-noticed and the townsfolk were beginning to talk. Rumors began to spread.

Stories or Waltz, himself, doing away with his absent partner. Backed into a corner, Waltz knew he must now come forth with the whole story.

But, he thought, there was one other choice. Instead of making known to the world his treasure site, he opted to depart Florence under the cover of darkness. Perhaps someday, he just might wish to return to the mine.

By the summer of 1871, Waltz had settled back into his Phoenix homestead, the image of Jacob Weiser's mutilated body still fresh in his mind. Here, within the security of his one-hundred, sixty acre estate he would mentally heal. He found himself beginning to drink heavily and could often be found in the local saloons buying drinks for the house and telling his wild stories to anyone who would lend an ear.

In the next few years his shock subsided, his courage rose and his bankroll fell. He felt uneasy about returning to the mountains but financial situations were forcing his hand.

By 1873, the United States Military had declared an all out war with the Apaches. Fort McDowell had been established near the Verde River and to the southeast, across the Superstitions, camps Pinal and Picket Post. Military trails had been paved through the mountains linking the three units. Waltz prayed their combined force would ultimately drive the savages far from his intended destination.

He would be overly cautious this trip. Taking only one pack burro, he would slip into the mountain from the southwestern range. He would chip out enough rock for one, quick load and be out before anyone could detect his presence. With hopes soaring, he set off.

By the evening of the fourth day he was standing atop a mountain range gazing across the canyon to the old cave where he and Weiser had once set up house-keeping. Looking around, he found he could trace the military roads to the east and west. To the southwest the tip of Weaver's Needle could be seen jutting up, above another, massive range. To the north, the peaks of four mountains highlighted the horizon. Waltz knew a short distance below from where he stood, he would find the shaft. But for now, with the threat of darkness approaching, Waltz would make camp for the night.

Daybreak found Waltz standing alongside the shaft. His first order of business was that of putting to rest the body of his old friend, Jacob Weiser. Weiser's body was buried alongside the graves of the two Mexicans that they had slain shortly before his death. Waltz stood a moment studying his private cemetary. Once the burial was completed, Waltz readied himself for the more fruitful work ahead.

With his lantern and rifle at the ready, Waltz began his decent into the mine. First he knew, he must check the hole for snakes and other creatures that may have taken up habitation in the shaft's lower recesses. He also realized he was alone, one mistake now would be fatal. If he were to slip and break a leg, there would be on one to rely on. A quick bullet to the head would be more merciful than the agonizing death from the bite of a snake or slowly dying from starvation. But today, luck would be with him, he reached the bottom of the shaft unhindered and re-confirmed the riches it contained.

In the years 1873 through 1878, Waltz quietly worked the location. At times he picked away at the shaft, at others he panned the flakes and pebbles from the pits in the canyon below. However, his age and health would not allow him to extract the metal in quantity.

During the winter months his house in the cave became his home away from home, as summer set in he and his burro would return to Phoenix. Always silent, he worked the gold only by hand and in constant fear. His frequent trips into Florence for supplies and to sell gold became too risky. People were remembering him and questions were again being asked. On one instance, Waltz tried bypassing the settlement, going on another sixty miles south, to sell his gold in Tucson. This one trip proved this township to be too far out of the way for his purposes.

Though hard and slow going, Waltz did manage to bring home enough gold to run his modest farm and keep up it's taxes, any excess spent on wild and exhuberant drinking binges. In 1875 he paid taxes on two-hundred, fifty dollars worth of personal property. Quite an amount for the time, as personal property did not include land owned.

The treasure trips went on until 1878, when Waltz became ill and was forced from his mountain retreat.

At the age of seventy, Waltz feared his last days were nearing. His treasure retrieving days seemed to be over and he found himself in dire need of medical attention. In anguish and desperation, he turned to his neighbor, Doctor Andrew Starrar. Starrar soon discovered Waltz to be penniless, the result of pouring his money into liquor and mismanaging his land. But Starrar, being the "friend" that he was, was able to reach an agreement with Waltz.

Starrar agreed to advance Waltz fifty dollars in cash and attend to his medical needs for the remainder of Waltz's life. In return,

Waltz signed over to Starrar everything he owned, land, cattle and crops. Even a debt owed Waltz by the estate of Ferdinand Madgeburg went to Starrar. Waltz was allowed to remain on the land and reap any profit he made from it.

For several years Waltz continued to live on the property, the sale of wheat being his main source of income. By 1881, he had recovered enough to join the few prospectors who were beginning to work the nearby area of Goldfield. Many times he considered returning to his gold mine, but realized the trip was too far and perilous for his health.

On October 11, 1882, Waltz registered to vote in the great Registry of Maricopa County. One year later, in the fall of 1883, Waltz felt confident he could endure one, final trip into the mountains.

Waltz returned from this endeavor somewhat successful. He believed he had returned with enough ore to see himself through his last days in comfort. Behind, he had concealed the opening of the shaft with rock and brush to keep it hidden on the outside chance he may possibly one day wish to return.

Once again with money in his pockets, the lure of the local saloon pulled him in. With his golden proof, he began spreading the tale of his latest adventure. Stories that fell upon the ears of two locals, Selso Grajalva and Pedro Ortega.

On the morning of June 18, 1884, the two Mexicans crept quietly up to the abode of Jacob Waltz. It was still dark outside and they had come unarmed, intent only on robbing the sleeping old man. Unknown to them, Waltz had spent many fearful nights growing accustomed to every minute sound that filled the air. Since the death of Weiser, Waltz had not found a truly peaceful sleep, at best only rest disturbed by visions of the past. Hence, the lightly sleeping old man became aware of the intruders before they had reached the door.

The two inexperienced thieves were caught off guard by the blast of Waltz's shotgun. Ortega lay lifeless on the ground as Grajalva fled in terror with Waltz close at his heels.

The next day the Arizona Gazette ran an article entitled "Four Murder". It stated that on June 19th, Justice of the Peace James Richards convened a coroners jury at the home of Jacob Waltz, investigating the murder of Pedro Ortega. Waltz, the only eye witness, claimed that he heard Ortega and Grajalva outside his home, fighting. He stated, he then heard a gunshot and ran from the house finding Ortega lying dead and Grajalva nowhere to be seen.

The article follows Waltz's testimony with the fact that a sheriff's deputy discovered that Waltz's shotgun was the murder weapon. Waltz's testimony was that he had not known his weapon had been fired. As Waltz was the only eye witness this left the jury to conclude that Grajalva had replaced the weapon in Waltz's home before fleeing. Although the story seemed contrived and ridiculous, Grajalva could not be found to refute it, therefore his guilt was concluded. And although suspision lingered on in the minds of his neighbors, Waltz was absolved of any guilt. Still many felt that some of Waltz's gold had changed hands that day for shortly afterwards Waltz was seen trading with the Mesa gold merchants.

Julia Corn was born in Louisiana December of 1862, the daughter of two german parents. On December 28, 1883 she married Emil W. Thomas in Colorado City, Texas. By 1884, she and her new husband had moved to Phoenix and established a confectionary business. It was here Jacob Waltz made her aquaintance.

Waltz and the young lady must have hit it off fairly well, for many times he donated his gold to help save her failing business. So much so that by 1886, when Starrar failed to pay the taxes on the property where Waltz lived, Waltz himself, could not save it. It appeared his charity and drink had once again caused his ruin. The property was sold on March 17, 1886 at a sheriffs auction.

The seventy-two year old Waltz however, did not find himself without at least one friend. Julia Thomas convinced her husband to let the old German move into the adobe shack behind their home. Here, Waltz would remain through two other disasters.

On, May 3, 1887, Mother Nature unleashed her fury in the form of the Bavispi earthquake. The entire central Arizona region was shook, bringing minor damage to the populated areas. But over the Superstition Mountains, huge, brown clouds of dust hung in the air, the major force of the quake being located there. How much damage it had done to Waltz's sacred area he would never know, for he would never see it again.

The second disaster, which would eventually stake the claim to Waltz's life, was also of Mother Nature's doing. In February of 1891, rain pounded the desert landscape, the saturated ground soaked up the moisture like a sponge but could hold no more. In the mountains to the east of Phoenix, water ran in torrents down the slopes, rushing through the canyons to the Salt River and swelling it to the point of bursting.

In Phoenix, people were sandbagging their homes in expectation of the raging water. The more concerned, including recently divorced Julia Thomas, sought refuge in the higher grounds of northern Phoenix. Waltz and the other, more stubborn were not willing to leave until absolutely necessary. Soon Waltz discovered, he had lingered too long.

On February 20th, the waters began racing through the town, steadily rising. Waltz found his only safe refuge in a tree just outside his dwelling. As the water continued it's momentum below, he watched as his adobe home was washed away in the thunderous onslaught.

For days he remained stranded, nestled in the tree, wet, hungry and near to death. On the third day the rains stopped, the deludge subsided and the inhabitants began to return and assess their damages. Waltz, overcome with fever, was rescued from his perch and taken to the home of Julia Thomas. Waltz had contracted pneumonia and now lay bedridden. During this time he had a few periods which indicated he might somehow pull through. In them he began to talk freely to

Julia about the location of his secret cache. At one point he even promised to lead her to it once he had fully recovered. Unfortunately for both of them he never did and on October 26, 1891 the Phoenix Daily Herald reported;

Jacob Waltz, aged 81 years died at 6 a.m. Sunday, October 25, 1891, and was buried at 10 o'clock this morning, from the residence of Mrs. J. D. Thomas, who had kindly nursed him through his last sickness. Deceased was a native of Germany and spent the last thirty years of his life in Arizona, mining part of the time, ranching and raising chickens. His honest, industrious, amiable character led Mrs. Thomas to care for him during his final days on earth, and he died with a blessing for her on his lips.

Following his death, others began to claim that they, too, had heard some of Waltz's deathbed revelations. Many, including Julia Thomas spent the better part of their remaining lives searching in vain to locate the Dutchman's lost mine.

Through the years the stories of those first "Lost Dutchman Mine" hunters have been handed down. Their clues, now almost a century old, have been diluted by time. As you will read in the next chapter, the most prominate and midleading clue to sift its way into the legend is that of Weaver's Needle. People have made it a focal point and lost fact to legend. Though there are many and sometimes conflicting clues today I have chosen to list the following as the most widely accepted.

Clue #1: It is difficult to find for it lies off all beaten paths.

Clue #2: From a deep northern canyon, it lies in a tributary running east and west.

Clue #3: From a two room house in the mouth of a cave, two-hundred yards across a gulch, on the mountain opposite, a concealed tunnel leads directly down to a wide vein of gold.

Clue #4: The gold is in a vein of rose quartz.

Clue #5: It is concealed with bushes and rocks.

Clue #6: You can not be seen from the military trail in the canyon below, but you could easily watch the trail.

Clue #7: Climb a short ways from a steep ravine and see a large peak.

Clue #8: A break in the mountains would allow the setting sun to shine through and glitter on the gold.

Clue #9: Find my house in the cave, my burro pen and Jacob Weisner's grave and you have found my mine.

Clue #10: I have my own personal cemetary.

CHAPTER IV

ADOLF RUTH

In 1912, the Peralta name was once again, added to the history of the Superstition Mountains. At this time, Dr. Erwin Ruth was serving as a federally appointed veterinarian in the area of the Texas-Mexican border. There, he had made the acquaintance of a former Mexican consul to the United States, by the name of Juan J. Gonzales. Gonzales, it seems, was about to be executed for his involvement in a revolution.

Ruth became close to Gonzales, who claimed to be a grandson of a Spanish miner named Peralta. Gonzales also claimed he possessed maps that would lead to long abandoned mines in California and Arizona. For the exchange of these maps, Ruth promised to care for the Mexican's family after his execution. Being no more than a curiosity to Ruth, he sent the maps off, to his father, Dr. Adolf Ruth.

The elder Ruth was fascinated by any lost mine story, so much so that he possessed a modest scrapbook into which went the Peralta maps. Here the maps remained until 1923, at which time, he began to search for the lost Peralta mine of California. Shortly, he returned home, a silver plate now implanted into his hip, the result of a broken bone incurred by a nasty fall while searching in the darkness for the lost treasure.

Unable to find the hidden riches, Ruth went back to his civil service position and remained with the government another eight years. Then in 1931, he retired and taking up another Peralta map, headed for Arizona.

In May, now puching sixty years of age, Ruth arrived in Phoenix. By June he was residing at "Tex" Barkley's Quarter Circle-U Ranch, at the foothills of the Superstitions.

Once there, he presented the map for Barkley's comments. Barkely studied the old map, which appeared to be more of a drawing of a location than a conventional map.

Depicted were two large peaks, bordering a gulley below. In the left hand peak a house in a cave was pictured and labled thus. The opposite peak displayed the location of a tunnel. Along a line, which was evident to be the canyon floor, several circles, with crosses in them, were labled "agua", the Spanish equivalent for water. The peak with the house in the cave and labled "La Sombrero", was then erroniously interpetted by Barkley to be the present day peak, Weaver's Needle.

Ruth, now having a definate landmark, found Barkley reluctant to guide him into the mountains for the sweltering heat of summer was upon them. So while Barkley was away on business, Ruth secretly persuaded two ranch hands, L. F. Purnell and Jack Keenan, to pack him into the wilderness.

On June 14th, Purnell and Keenan helped Ruth to make camp at Willow Springs and with the promise of returning with more supplies later, left the old man on his own.

Several days later, when Barkley returned and found Ruth was already in the mountains, he became worried. On June 20th he set out with the intent of talking Ruth out of the Superstitions until the cooler seasons engulfed the area.

Barkley rode into Ruth's camp and found it empty, the old man was nowhere to be found. The local authorities were notified and a search was begun. But it would not be until December of that year before his skeletal remains would begin to be found, in West Boulder Canyon.

Found among the pieces of clothing were the hand drawn map which he had shown to Barkley and a note in Ruth's own handwriting.

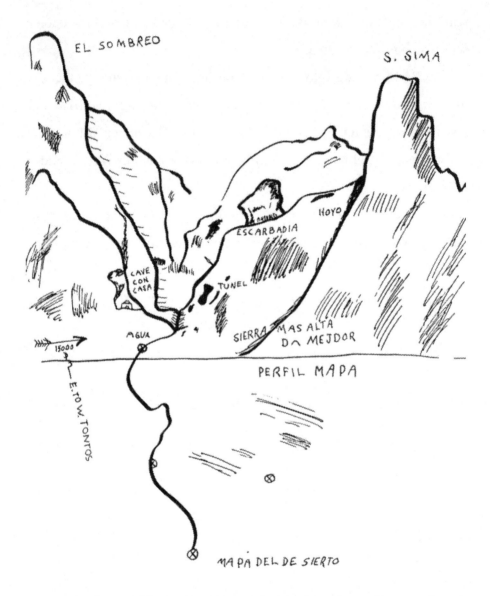

"It lies within an imaginary circle, else where diameter is not more than about five miles and whose center is marked by Weavers' Needle, about 2500 feet high- amoung a confusion of lesser peaks and mountain masses of bastic rock. The first gorge on the south side from the western end of the range, they found a monumented trail which led them northward over a lofty ridge thence downward past Sombreo Butte into a long canyon is running morth and finally to a subtary canyon very deep and rocky and densely wooded with a contiguous thicket of scrub oak.

Veni, Vidi, Vici

About 200 feet across from the cave."

Somehow Ruth had discovered a portion of the old "monumented" Peralta Trail that wove its' way through the mountains into New Mexico. He had followed its' path as far as the cliff dwelling and discovered its' secrets. Then, trying to return to his base camp, he probably became lost. Of his death one might suppose his age and unfimiliararity with the diverse mountain ranges led to him becoming lost, dying of exposure to the unrelenting summer sun, thirst or perhaps even the fatal bite from a deadly reptile.

Many stories, with their various details, have been written concerning the exploites and mysterious death of Adolp Ruth. Though interesting, they bear no true value in uncovering the mystery of the Lost Dutchman Mine. Or primary concern is the map, itself.

Gonzales and Ruth proported it to show the location of an old Peralta mine, of Spanish origin. It is remarkable that it equivocally fits the description of Waltz's mine; the house in the cave and the shaft being on opposite sides of a gulley. It has been handed down with the Dutchman legend that Waltz, himself, claimed to be working old Spanish diggings. Even the directions Ruth left lead to the same location I earlier identified as the Lost Dutchman Mine and match the clues of Jacob Waltz to the exact detail.

The conclusion that can only be found is that they are one in the same.

SUMMARY

For many years, Superstition Mountain history has been passed down, each new generation adding to and twisting the facts. The result is the many and diversified tales and legends we have today. But, as most legends have some basis in fact, so it is with these ancient mountains. These facts are simple and, when brought together, the Lost Dutchman Legend stands as real and tangible as the mountains themselves.

As we have previously shown, there *were* Jesuit Priests in the area of the Gila River as early as 1701. They *were* expelled for utilizing their Indian converts in slave mining operations. The Peralts Stone Maps and Trail Markers *are* authentic. The trail *can* be traced from the Gila Mission to the heart shaped stone overlooking the four mines. Not only Mexican legend, but Indian history tells the tale of the Peralta massacre.

Federal records and claim deeds of the 1800's, bearing the name of Jacob Waltz, *can* be verified. His grave in Phoenix can be visited today. Recorded tax records indicate Waltz was not always a poor man. Fact, after fact, after fact, leads to the only logical conclusion...The Superstition Mountains do contain a lost gold mine.

As to its whereabout, I draw your attention to a location in Rogers Canyon. Here, among the hidden ruins of the past, I have unraveled the fabulous mystery. I have found the house in the cave, the tunnel, and the hole pictured in the Peralta-Ruth map. Even the terrain of the area fits perfectly, without deviation. The rugged floor of the canyon, etched and deeply pitted by raging winter floods is also here as on the map.

Add to all this my own discoveries…just below the house in the cave I have found what I believe to be the Dutchman's burro pen made from stones stacked one upon the other. Also, down the canyon, south of the site, a large, a horse shaped rock formation stares back to the north.

I have stood at the mine's entrance and gazed in beyond huge boulders and debris to see several feet inside. Pieces of rose quartz lay scattered all around and traces can be seen in the mine's walls. Either erosion or the great earthquake of the 1880's has brought down part of mountain above, partially obstructing the tunnel inside. However, the stout of heart can still cautiously make his way into the pits dark, cold recesses.

On June 10, 1965, Public Land Order #3684 went into effect. 320 acres of Superstition Range were set aside as a public landmark and recreation area. No motor vehichles are allowed anywhere on the reserve. As of January 1, 1984, the entire 125,000 acre Wilderness Area was effected. As a result, the Federal Government now denies *any* mining or the filing of claims. Forest Service rangers now patrol and protect against any would-be prospectors. But as for me……

Veni, vidi, vici.

Charles H. Huckabay

About the Author

The author Charles Hoyt Huckabay, grew up around the superstition mountains and found many of the unknown areas that are there. Has a great knowledge of the history of Arizona and surrounding areas. Has been involved in training horses, rodeo, team roping and riding horse back into the wilderness all his life.

CPSIA information can be obtained
at www.ICGtesting.com
Printed in the USA
BVOW08s0844150418

513425BV00001BA/256/P